THE GOOD FRIENDS CLUB

**story and pictures
by Bob Barner**

HOUGHTON MIFFLIN COMPANY   BOSTON

Atlanta   Dallas   Geneva, Illinois   Palo Alto   Princeton   Toronto

"This is not my day," said Dog.

"I know how you feel," said Monkey,
"Everyone feels like that sometimes.
 You need a good laugh!"

"I don't feel much like laughing," said Dog.

"Come to the Good Friends Club," said Monkey.
"You'll feel like laughing there."

Monkey and Dog went to
the Good Friends Club.
Everyone was there!

"Dog needs a good laugh," said Monkey.
"Let's help Dog feel happy again."

"I'll sing!" shouted Rabbit.

Rabbit was singing,
and everyone was laughing.
Everyone but Dog.

"I'll dance!" shouted Turtle.

Turtle was dancing,
and everyone was laughing.
Everyone but Dog.

"I'll tell jokes!" shouted Duck.

Duck was telling jokes,
and everyone was laughing.
Everyone but Dog.

"I know!" said Monkey.
"I think we should all sing
and dance and tell jokes!"

Everyone was singing and
dancing and telling jokes,
and everyone was laughing.
Everyone but Dog.

But then, all at once, Dog
said, "HA-HA."
Then Dog said it again, and
then again!
Dog was laughing too!

"HA-HA!" laughed Dog.
"HA-HA! HA-HA! HA-HA!"

"HA-HA!" everyone laughed.
"HA-HA! HA-HA! HA-HA!"

"What good friends you are!" said Dog.
"You helped me feel happy again.
Hurray for the Good Friends Club!"

"Not the Good Friends Club," said Monkey.
"Now the name is the HA-HA Club!"
Then everyone laughed, "HA-HA! HA-HA!"